No one can command his fart . . .

I plopped down in my chair, and the whoopee cushion did its thing. But that wasn't enough for me. I mean, if you have to sit on a whoopee cushion, you might as well make the loudest sound possible, right?

The whoopee cushion went *Bllaat!*

And I went *F-f-f-BLAT-BLAT-BLAT!*

Looks of absolute horror from everyone in the room! I started to giggle.

Then I saw Roy. He was clenching his fist at me.

"That whiff better not blow this way, funny guy," he said.

Suddenly I stopped laughing. Because as you know, you may be able to fart on command, but no one can command his fart.

I think it was Shakespeare who said that. Or else Jim Carrey.

I could see the fart's progress. One face after another crinkled in disgust as my deadly whiff blew past.

It was heading straight for Roy!

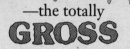

MUCUS MANSION

BY
PAT POLLARI

BANTAM BOOKS
NEW YORK·TORONTO·LONDON·SYDNEY·AUCKLAND

RL 4, age 008-012

MUCUS MANSION
A Bantam Book / July 1996

*Barf-O-Rama™ and the Barf-O-Rama Logo™ are
trademarks of Daniel Weiss Associates, Inc.*

*Produced by Daniel Weiss Associates, Inc.
33 West 17th Street
New York, NY 10011*

ISBN: 0-553-48408-7

Published simultaneously in the United States and Canada

Bantam Books are published by Bantam Books, a division of Bantam
Doubleday Dell Publishing Group, Inc. Its trademark, consisting of the
words "Bantam Books" and the portrayal of a rooster, is Registered in U.S.
Patent and Trademark Office and in other countries. Marca Registrada.
Bantam Books, 1540 Broadway, New York, New York 10036.

PRINTED IN THE UNITED STATES OF AMERICA

OPM   0 9 8 7 6 5 4 3 2 1

To Michael

ONE

I should have known old Uncle Elmont would have one last trick up his sleeve. But I really figured he had played his last disgusting prank.

What with him being dead and all.

I mean, normally, dead people don't do much of anything, right?

There I was, Seth Cooke, standing in the front of the church surrounded by all of Uncle Elmont's relatives. I was wearing my incredibly uncomfortable suit. It's scratchy, it's hot, it's tight. And the shoes? I swear they're made out of steel.

But it was a funeral, so I had to dress up. My little sister, Annette, was standing next to me. She was dressed up, too. But she seemed to actually enjoy it.

So, anyway, there we were. Uncle Elmont was in a wooden casket covered with flowers. The pastor was saying what a wonderful man he was.

"Elmont was a man among men. A gentle man. A kind man. A decent man . . ."

I'm not saying it was a lie, because we all know pastors don't lie. But I don't think anyone in that church believed a single word the pastor was saying.

Let's just say that Uncle Elmont was not popular.

Not popular in the same way that rotten eggs are not a popular choice for breakfast.

Not popular in the same way that sewer surfing is not a popular sport.

Not popular in the same way that going to the dentist and having your molars drilled without Novocain is not a popular thing to do.

Let me put it this way: There were people who couldn't stand Uncle Elmont. And then there were people who really, *really* couldn't stand Uncle Elmont.

So while the pastor was saying what a great guy Uncle Elmont had been, everyone in the church was kind of rolling their eyes or snickering.

Of course, even though they all hated him, everyone showed up for the funeral. Why? Duh. Because he was rich.

RICH!

So rich he had one servant to cook his food, another servant to eat it for him, and a third one to go to the bathroom eight hours later.

Okay, that's not totally true. I kind of made that up. It's a joke. When I grow up, I want to be a comedian. My parents think I'm nuts. But that's because they have no sense of humor.

None. Neither do my grandparents. Or anyone else in our family.

See, by some weird twist of fate, the only two people in our entire family who had any sense of humor were me and Uncle Elmont. It gave us something in common.

So, anyway, there we are, standing in the church, listening to the pastor tell us how generous and kind Uncle Elmont was, when we heard the noise.

Pop!

A definite pop.

I kind of glanced down at Annette. She shrugged.

Then another pop. A double.

Pop! Pop!

It was strange, because the first thing that came to my mind was: fart. It sounded exactly like a fart. Only kind of muffled, like one of those farts where the farter is trying not to let anyone know he's farting? You know how a person in the process of gassing while they're sitting down will sometimes kind of lean over to one side? They're hoping it will be a stealth fart and no one will know who fired the deadly flatus? But then, even though they've leaned over, the fart refuses to go ninja, and instead it turns into a squeezer or a popper?

Pop! Pop! Pop!

It was definitely the sound of a fart. A climbing multipopper, to be exact.

I may only be eleven, but I know farts. I'm kind of an expert. And this sounded a lot like a climbing multipopper—a multipopper that starts off slow, then gets faster and louder.

"Someone's firing fartillery," I whispered to Annette.

She rolled her eyes. Like the rest of the family, she has no sense of humor.

POP! POP! POP! POPOPOPOPOP!

"It's coming from the casket!" someone cried out.

They were right. It seemed incredible, but Uncle Elmont was farting inside his casket. Farting like he was trying to blow off the lid. He was farting up a farticane.

"*Oooooooohhhhh!*" someone moaned. My mom, I think.

Some other people yelped a little, too. The preacher stopped talking, that's for sure.

POPOPOPOPOP!

"Oh, my!" my dad moaned.

Then Uncle Elmont went tuba on us. He went into total pootaphone mode.

BLAAAT! BLAAAT! BLAAAAAAAAAAT!

I was just grateful there was a lid on that casket. I mean, Uncle Elmont was releasing so much poopfume that if it had gotten out, we would have all been gassed unconscious.

BLAAAAAT!

It wasn't stopping. I mean, it was *not* stopping!

Now people were starting to look nervous. I sure was. Because, see, I was near the front. That casket was only about ten feet away. You need more than ten feet between yourself and that much poopfume. I believe the Environmental Protection Agency recommends at least fifty yards.

Then, just as Uncle Elmont released another blast from beyond the grave, the casket started to rumble.

It shook.

It rattled.

It was moving like there was an earthquake, which could only mean one thing:

"It's gonna blow!" I yelled.

At that moment: *BOOOOOM!*

The lid flew off the casket.

"Eeeeeee!"

Men screamed like babies.

"Aaaarrrrgghh!"

There was a stampede toward the door. But too late. Green, awful goo, the exact consistency of snot, exploded out of the casket.

"DEATH SNOT!" I yelled.

Great globs of the mucus flew through the air. It landed in the flowers. It landed on the pastor. It landed on my cousin Roy, which was the only good thing.

And a wad of it landed on my face.

You have no idea what an entire church full of well-dressed people, terrified of farting corpses and covered with death snot looks like.

It's not a pretty sight. But it *is* funny.

Right then I got it. No one else got it, but I did.

By the way, did I mention why everyone hates Uncle Elmont? Because he is the world's grossest, most disgusting, most repulsive practical joker.

From his casket Uncle Elmont had just made his last gross-out practical joke.

Or . . . was it his last?

TWO

"He had to leave the money to *someone*, Jessica," my dad said to my mom.

"Don't be so sure, Roger," my mom said. "That rotten old man probably donated it all to some unworthy cause. Just to cheat us out of our share!"

It was the day after the funeral. We were all in the car, heading for some lawyer's office. Supposedly we were going to find out about Uncle Elmont's will. A will is something that tells people what you want to do with your stuff after you're dead.

"Knowing Uncle Elmont, he probably donated it all to the ISF: Institute for the Study of Farts," I said. "Or maybe WCU: Whoopee Cushion University. Or maybe to the MOM: Museum of Mucus."

I waited for the laughter. Naturally my parents just stared at me. My mom said, "Seth, don't say fart."

"That boy has a little of Uncle Elmont in him," my father growled.

It always kind of hurt my feelings when they said that. Just because I had a sense of humor, that didn't mean I was like Uncle Elmont.

Not at all.

Annette just gave me that look she has that says, Why did I have to get such a dweeb for a big brother?

"We could certainly use that money," my dad said. He was gripping the steering wheel real tight. "There could be layoffs coming at work. I could lose my job. But if we got a few million of Elmont's money, well, I could march in there and tell my boss to—"

"Hush, Roger," my mom interrupted him. "Not in front of the kids."

"I'm just saying, we could use the money."

We parked in the underground garage beneath this big office building. Then we rode the elevator to the eighteenth floor.

The lawyer's office was very fancy. There were all kinds of chrome and leather chairs and all.

10

A bunch of people were already there, sitting in leather chairs. Mostly they were the same crowd that was at Uncle Elmont's funeral. Everyone was a relative of one kind or another—cousins, aunts, uncles, great-granduncles, and so on. My horrible cousin Roy was there. So was my creepy, annoying cousin Sondra.

I pretended to smile at Sondra and tried not to look at Roy. Roy has been torturing me at every family get-together since I was born.

The lawyer was like eighty years old. He was so old, he was dusty. He sat behind the desk and looked us over as we came in.

There were four empty chairs over to one side. My mom sat down first.

Bllaaat!

It sounded like a fart. But I knew better. I mean, come on, Seth Cooke fooled by a whoopee cushion? I don't think so.

But my mom turned completely red.

"It's just a whoopee cushion," I told her. "There's probably one on every chair."

"I'm afraid you are correct, young man," the dusty lawyer said. "It is one of the terms of Elmont's will. At the reading of the will each person shall be made to simu-late a gaseous eruption by the placing of

11

their posteriors on a so-called whoopee cushion."

"Well, I am not sitting on a whoopee cushion!" my father said.

"That is your choice," the lawyer intoned. "But if you do not sit on the whoopee cushion and thus simulate a gaseous eruption, I'm afraid you cannot inherit anything from Elmont's will."

"You have to play the pootaphone, Dad," I said.

"So the old man wants to humiliate us even from beyond the grave," my dad fumed. "Wasn't that spectacle at the funeral enough?"

But then Dad did what he had to do: He lined his hinder up with the chair and sat down.

Bllaaat!

I had to bite my tongue to keep from laughing. Everyone else in the room thought it was just awful. Me, I thought it was kind of funny.

I plopped down in my chair and the whoopee cushion did its thing. But that wasn't enough for me. I mean, if you have to sit on a whoopee cushion, you might as well make the loudest sound possible, right? So . . . I'd had oatmeal for breakfast that morning. I don't know why, but oatmeal always gets me majorly inflated.

The whoopee cushion went *Bllaat!*

And I went *F-f-f-BLAT-BLAT-BLAT!*

Looks of absolute horror from everyone in the room! I started to giggle so hard, I was doubled over.

Then I saw Roy. He was clenching his fist at me.

"That whiff better not blow this way, funny guy," he said.

Suddenly I stopped laughing. Because as you know, you may be able to fart on command, but no one can command his fart.

I think it was Shakespeare who said that. Or else Jim Carrey.

I could see the fart's progress. One face after another crinkled in disgust as my deadly whiff blew past.

It was heading straight for Roy!

THREE

My fart and Roy's nose were on a collision course!

I hate to admit it, but I'm a little afraid of Roy. He's fourteen and built like a football player. And he's about as smart as AstroTurf.

My great-uncle Darren's nose wrinkled in disgust as my fart rolled over him. There was only one place left for my traveling whiff. It was going to hit Roy!

Three seconds to impact!

I looked left. There was a window! "I think we could use some fresh air," I yelled. I jumped up. I leapt over my aunt Talia. I tripped. I hit the ground and rolled back up on my feet.

One second to impact!

15

The window flew open. I could practically see my gaseous eruption hesitate. Then it was sucked back by the force of the breeze.

Everyone was staring at me. "I . . . uh . . . I like fresh air." I sat down again. *BLAAT!*

"Now, can we get on with this?" That was my mom's brother George. He's Roy's father.

"Yes, we may now proceed with the reading of the will," the lawyer said. "But first, would anyone care for a beverage? Coffee? Tea? Lemonade?"

It's amazing how dumb people can be when they have no sense of humor. I mean, give me a break! After the whoopee cushion incident Uncle Elmont's lawyer decides to offer you a beverage? How dumb do you have to be not to realize something is up?

But of course everyone said, "Sure, I'll have a tea, a coffee, a lemonade," or whatever.

The lawyer's assistant brought in the drinks. I said, "No, thanks."

"Everyone comfortable now?" the lawyer asked. "Fine, then we'll proceed. In this case the will is not a written document. Instead it is a videotape."

"So we'll have to see the old pirate one more time?" my dad grumbled.

"Exactly," the lawyer agreed. He picked up a remote control on his desk and pointed it at the bookshelf. The bookshelf opened up and a TV appeared. It was very cool.

The TV came on and there he was: Uncle Elmont.

Uncle Elmont is old. Or *was* old, anyway. He was at least as old as the lawyer. In fact, he and the lawyer looked a little alike. Except the lawyer had gray hair and Uncle Elmont was almost totally bald, and Uncle Elmont had a mustache and wore glasses, unlike the lawyer.

But I guess most really old people look about the same.

Anyway, there was Uncle Elmont, looking like he usually did, except that he was sitting in a bathtub.

I mean, it was okay because you could only see him from the chest up. But still, old men should not be going around without their shirts on. There should be some kind of law against it.

So there was Uncle Elmont with his saggy old-man skin and his droopy mustache that was always decorated with little bits of whatever he'd had to eat, sitting in a bathtub holding a yellow rubber duck and smoking a big fat cigar.

He was grinning at the camera.

"Well, hello, everyone," he said. "If it isn't my loving family, all assembled together."

"Yeah, right," someone muttered.

"I hope you all enjoyed the service yesterday. By the way, I think you can get those death snot stains out of your clothes with a little soda water and a brush. Ha-HA!"

There was a kind of dangerous muttering from everyone in the room. No one wanted to be reminded of the death snot.

Then it occurred to me—why would Uncle Elmont call it death snot? I thought I just made that up. Oh, well, maybe it was just a case of great minds thinking alike.

"Anyway," Uncle Elmont went on, "you're all sitting there very glad that I'm dead and anxious to learn what I'm going to do with all my money, while I am just sitting here in my tub making bubbles, if you know what I mean. Ha-HA!" He got a look of concentration on his face. Then I heard a definite sound of bubbles in the bathwater.

"Disgusting!" my great-aunt Lillith said.

"Are you surprised that he would be disgusting right to the end?" her husband asked.

I had to bite my tongue again to keep from laughing.

"Yes, I'm just sitting here, thinking of all of you," Uncle Elmont said as he puffed on his fat cigar. "Sitting and making bubbles in the bathwater. I wonder if bath farts give the water a special flavor? Hmmm. I wonder?"

Then he grinned right at the camera. "Well, *does* it give the water a special flavor?"

I had a bad feeling about what he was going to say next.

"I mean, all of you should know. See, that coffee and tea and lemonade you're drinking was made from this *bathwater!* Ha-HA!"

FOUR

"Fartwater *coffee!*" Uncle Elmont crowed gleefully.

SPEW!

It was simultaneous mass spewage! Coffee spurted from the mouth of Uncle Tony and Cousin Freddy and Third-cousin Janette.

"Fartwater *tea!*" Uncle Elmont cackled.

SPEW!

Tea sprayed from the red-lipsticked mouth of Great-aunt Lillith.

"*Aaargh!*"

"*Bleaaah!*"

"Fartwater *lemonade!*" Uncle Elmont cried. "Ha-HA!"

Lemonade gushed from the mouths of my cousin Roy and my little sister.

I ducked down in the chair and let the spew storm blow past.

It was a spew monsoon!

"That monster!" someone yelled.

"That rotten old man!" someone else said.

And I can't even tell you what my own mother said. But basically everyone was pretty upset. It was a good thing Uncle Elmont was dead. Because I think if he'd been around, all my relatives would have killed him.

And they weren't exactly happy with me, either. See, I was the only one who didn't have a fartwater beverage. I was the only one who wasn't gacking and groaning and rubbing their tongues with their sleeves like they were trying to clean it off.

But at least I had the sense not to laugh. For once. I mean, professional comedians talk about a tough room. That means a bunch of people who really, really are not in the mood to laugh.

Well, let me tell you, the lawyer's office was a tough room right then. Everyone was soaked from the spew storm.

"It's an outrage!" I yelled, trying to get into the spirit. I jumped up out of my chair. "We should all just walk right out of here. We don't need Uncle Elmont's money this much! Let's go!"

To my surprise, no one agreed with me. Instead they all got silent and kind of sullen. So I sat back down. Which naturally made my whoopee cushion go *BLLAAT!*

The lawyer started the videotape up again.

"Ahhhh. Ha-HA, I wish I could be there to see what just happened!" He was laughing so hard, he was crying. "But I can imagine it. As for me, I never indulge in coffee or tea. I find a nice glass of apple juice in the morning sets me up nicely. Be that as it may, now we must get on to business."

Suddenly the picture was different. Now Uncle Elmont was in a business suit, looking very stiff and very formal in his office. His entire expression was changed. I'd never seen him look so normal.

"My dear family," he began, "the time has come to get serious."

"It's about time," my dad said.

"The time has come to tell you what I plan to do with my great fortune."

Everyone in the room moved forward. I looked around. It was kind of creepy. Like a bunch of vultures checking out a piece of roadkill.

"Well, I won't make you wait any longer," Uncle Elmont said. "What I plan to do with my fortune . . . which amounts to something like a hundred million dollars . . . is split it evenly among all the children of our family: Roy, Sondra, Tyler, Rosemary, Annette, and Seth."

It was amazing. It was like you could actually *hear* everyone's brain adding up and dividing and multiplying as they tried to figure out what this meant for each family.

"There is only one small thing I ask in return . . . ," Uncle Elmont said.

"Uh-oh," my mom said.

"Here it comes," Great-aunt Lillith said.

"Just one little thing I require," Uncle Elmont said. "Each of the children I have just named must spend one complete twenty-four-hour period staying in my mansion. Any child who leaves will lose his portion of the inheritance. And the ones who stay will split the percentage of the child who leaves."

Suddenly the serious expression slipped just a bit. He was trying hard not to laugh. "If only one child stays the entire night, that child and his family will inherit *everything*."

Total, dead silence.

No one moved. No one said anything.

But then I saw Roy's eyes turn to stare at me.

I had a very bad feeling about this.

FIVE

I guess it's time for me to explain something to you.

I've told you that Uncle Elmont and I were the only two people in my family who have any sense of humor. And I've told you that some of the things Uncle Elmont did made me laugh. So you're probably thinking that I was a big fan of Uncle Elmont.

You'd be wrong. See, I was Uncle Elmont's favorite victim. He would pull practical jokes on everyone, from kids to really old adults. But when he pulled a trick on me, he always did something especially gross.

Let me give you an example. This was a few years ago when I was pretty young. I was in the junior Christmas pageant at our church. I was one of the wise men. You know, the guys who brought gold, frankincense, and myrrh. I was the wise man with the myrrh. Whatever myrrh is. I never did find out.

It was kind of a big thing to me. My family was all there in the audience. Some of my school friends were there. Everyone was dressed up and all.

So, anyway, I'm standing around offstage waiting for my time to go on. I'm wearing this dorky outfit of gold robes. And I have this turban I'm supposed to put on, only I have it sitting in the corner with my box of myrrh.

And who suddenly shows up backstage beside me? Uncle Elmont.

"Hey, Sethie boy, pretty exciting, huh?" he asks me.

I say, "I guess so, Uncle Elmont."

"Your first time onstage."

"That's right."

"I guess you're a little nervous."

I nodded.

Uncle Elmont smiled. "It would be a shame if anything went wrong while you were out there, huh?"

By this time, even though I was pretty

young, I was starting to think "Hmm, there is something strange going on here. Why is Uncle Elmont hanging around back here bugging me?"

"It's almost time for me to go out," I said. I looked around. My myrrh wasn't there. It was this little silver box, although actually the "silver" was just tinfoil crumpled over a cigar box.

"Where's my myrrh?" I was starting to panic. "And where's my turban?" I could hear the other actors out on the stage. They were getting to the point where the three of us wise men were supposed to go and say our lines. "I can't go out without my myrrh and my turban!"

"Is this what you're looking for?" Uncle Elmont asked. He was holding a tinfoil-covered box and a turban.

I thought he'd hidden them just to make me nervous. I pretended to think it was funny. "Very funny, Uncle Elmont," I said.

"Not *yet*, it isn't," he muttered. "Ha-HA!"

I didn't have time to think about what he was saying. I snatched up the silver box. I slapped the turban on my head.

If I had been paying attention right then . . .

but I wasn't. I was too worried about getting out on the stage and delivering my lines.

But if I *had* been paying attention, I would have noticed that this turban was heavier than it should have been. And it was bigger. And I would have noticed the box was heavier, too.

But like I said, I wasn't paying attention.

"Cue wise men!" the pageant director said. That meant me and the other two wise men were supposed to go out onstage.

The three of us walked out, kind of nervous, kind of unsure. Mary and Joseph and some kids playing shepherds were already out there. One of Annette's dolls was in the manger.

The first wise man opened his box and said, "I bring unto thee a gift of most precious gold!"

The second wise man opened his box and said, "I bring unto thee a gift of fragrant frankincense!"

I opened my box and said, "I bring unto thee a gift of . . . *poop?*"

The entire audience gasped.

I turned and looked out at my mom and dad in the audience. I showed them the box. "It's poop! It's a Lassie loaf!"

And it was. It was dog poop. From a poodle, if that makes any difference. Trust me, even though I was little, I knew poop when I saw it.

Just then a loud siren went off.

Waa-AAAA-aaaa-AAA . . .

It seemed to be coming from right over my head. It scared me half to death.

I jerked at the noise.

I jerked and about half of my "myrrh" went flying. It flew through the air. It turned somersaults. It landed in the front row of seats.

Right in the lap of my cousin Roy.

Cousin Roy was not really happy about having a load of moist canine buttwurst dropped on his lap. So he jumped up on the stage.

"I'm gonna pound you!" he shouted.

I ran. The siren in my turban was still wailing. I was still carrying my silver box. And now I was running like a lunatic around the stage, screaming, "I bring thee the gift of myrrh!"

"I'm gonna POUND you!"

"I bring thee the gift of myrrh!"

"You're DEAD!"

And while I was running, the rest of the poodle doo was flying in chunks this way and that.

Of course Uncle Elmont was over on the side of the stage, laughing so hard he was crying.

Ever since then two things have changed in my life.

First, Roy has really, *really* not liked me.

Second, I have really, *really* not trusted Uncle Elmont.

Oh, and there's a third thing, too. They don't let me in the annual Christmas pageant.

SIX

It was the fatal day. It was early morning. Sondra and her parents dropped by before breakfast to say that we should all stick together and not turn against each other. She said it would be bad karma to fight among ourselves. Karma. That's the kind of thing Sondra talks about.

I had no idea what karma was, but I didn't think Roy would be interested in sticking together, bad karma or not. I was pretty sure he would do his best to get rid of me and the others so he could have all the money to himself.

"How bad could it be?" Cousin Sondra wondered as we walked her parents to the front door.

I rolled my eyes. "Let's see—it's Uncle Elmont we're talking about. How bad could it be? It could be as bad as a Yanni concert. It could be as bad as reruns of *Good Times*. It could be as bad as accidentally eating a box of laxatives and then going on a camping trip with nothing but poison ivy for toilet paper."

Sondra shook her head. "You know, you and Uncle Elmont deserve each other. But aren't you forgetting the fact that he's dead?"

"He was dead when he got us with death snot and fartwater lemonade, too," I pointed out.

"I think you actually kind of liked Uncle Elmont," Sondra said.

I patted my dog, Ranger's, head. "I wish I could bring you, boy," I said. "You'd take care of Roy, wouldn't you?" Actually Ranger is kind of a small dog, so I wasn't sure how much he could do against Roy, but at least he barks loudly.

Sondra and her folks took off.

Watching her drive away, I had a bad feeling. Twenty-four hours of Uncle Elmont and Roy. I would have preferred to stay home and scrub the toilet bowl.

But what was I going to say to my folks?

Sorry, Mom and Dad, but I just don't think I'm interested in millions of dollars?

Yeah, right.

Besides, it was supposed to be *all* the kids. Which meant my annoying little sister, Annette, had to go, too. And I couldn't let her be braver or tougher than I was.

But I have to tell you, on that Saturday morning when I got up and got ready to stay at Uncle Elmont's house, I was not a happy kid.

My parents tried to be cool about it. They didn't say, "Seth, we'll KILL you if you lose us that money!"

Maybe they were *thinking* it. But they didn't say it.

Actually, my mom and dad are both all right. I knew they'd still love me if I messed up. Kind of.

"Eat your breakfast," my mom said. "It's your favorite: scrambled eggs and ham."

"It's great, Mom," I said. "Only you made about ten pounds of it."

"You need to keep up your strength," she said. "A good hearty breakfast will help get you through the day. Through the *twenty-four*-hour day. Yes, I'll bet a person could just

33

about go a full *twenty-four* hours on one really hearty breakfast—"

"Um, Mom?" I interrupted. "I think I'll eat a little more."

After breakfast we drove over to Uncle Elmont's house. I guess it's called an estate, actually. I mean there's all this land around it with trees and ponds and stuff. The driveway is practically a mile long.

As we pulled up, two cars were already parked there.

"Tyler and Rosemary are already here," I pointed out. "And there's Sondra."

We parked and got out. It was chilly because it was so early. The sky was gray. The house was gray. Everyone's face looked gray.

Suddenly I heard a loud grinding of gravel.

I spun around.

There was a car coming straight at me!

I jumped out of the way. The car slammed to a stop. Roy was inside, grinning at me. His father, George, was behind the wheel.

"Hey, what are you doing, you lunatic?" my father yelled.

"Sorry," George said. But he was grinning the same nasty grin as Roy.

I think my dad and George might have

34

gotten into a fight right there, but then the door of the house swung slowly open. The lawyer appeared in the doorway.

"I see everyone has arrived," he said. "Good. The twenty-four hours begin as soon as the children are all inside the house."

"How do we know something terrible isn't going to happen to our kids?" Tyler's mother yelled.

The lawyer just raised an eyebrow. "They will be offered food, and they will have beds for the night. They will not be . . . physically harmed. Elmont was not some sort of monster. And I will be here." The lawyer checked his watch. "Eight o'clock. It is time."

I felt pretty nervous right at that moment. I don't want to sound like a wimp or anything, but I hadn't spent any time away from home.

But I had to be strong. I had to be strong for my parents. And for Annette.

I took Annette's hand and squeezed it. I figured even though we don't get along, we should try and stick together.

"Don't be scared," I said.

"Me? I'm not the one who's scared. Roy doesn't hate *me*. You're the one whose hand is all sweaty from being nervous. You're the one who better watch out," she said.

Good old Annette. She's always very supportive. I let go of her hand. "You should just stay out here with Mom. I don't want to have to baby-sit you."

"Just deal with it, Seth."

"Well, okay, let's go," I said. I didn't want a big huggy-kissy scene with my mom. So I just yanked Annette along with me toward the front door.

"Are you as excited about this as I am?" Sondra asked me as we all crowded up by the door. She's thirteen and kind of pretty in a strange way that involves multiple earrings.

"Excited?" I said doubtfully. "I mean, we could use the money and all, I guess. I'm excited about that."

"No, no." Sondra shook her head. "That's not what I mean. It's just so weird. I mean, a dead guy's house? We have to stay all night in a dead guy's house."

"What are you saying?"

She smiled her slightly creepy Sondra smile. "I'm saying, what if it's haunted? Haunted by the ghost of Uncle Elmont?"

This idea had not occurred to me. I was just worried about Roy pounding on me. I hadn't thought about anything supernatural.

We stepped inside. We all fell silent. That's the way Uncle Elmont's house is. It's the kind of place that makes you fall silent.

We were in a huge open room. The ceiling was so high, you could barely see it. The walls were heavy, dark wood. They were all carved and covered with little curlicues and stuff. There were strange old paintings in gold frames. Paintings of old people that seemed to be staring down at us with very realistic eyes.

And I noticed there were various doors. All closed.

"There are no such things as ghosts," I told Sondra.

She looked around with eyes that were glittering with excitement. "Maybe there are ghosts and maybe there aren't," she said. "But I'll tell you one thing: If there are ghosts, this is exactly the kind of place you would find them."

SLAM!

Suddenly the door slammed shut behind us.

It was totally dark. So dark, I couldn't see my hand in front of my face.

And then . . . the stench. The stench!

The *STENCH!*

SEVEN

"A*aaargh!*"
      "Help us! HELP us!"

The stench rolled out in a wave. A gagging, putrefying wave. The smell washed over us. Odor filled our nostrils.

Then I felt something land on my head. It was soft. Soft but crusty. Then there were more of them. In the dark I couldn't *see* anything.

But I could *smell*.

"What is it?" Tyler cried out. I can always recognize his voice. He goes to one of those snooty private schools where they make you talk like you have a bad cold and you're about to sneeze. "That smell! Oh, oh! The horror!"

"Seth, what's happening?" Annette screamed. "I . . . I can't breathe!"

The soft things were still falling all around me. They landed on my head and my shoulders. I brushed them off, but more landed.

"Wait," I said. I tried to concentrate, but it wasn't easy. "I think I know what that smell is. If I could just concentrate without . . . g-g-gagging up breakfast."

But it was almost impossible. The horrible smell seeped into my brain. It made me crazy! My stomach was on its way to my throat.

It was just too horrible!

"I know what it is, too," Rosemary wailed. "It's awful! It's morbific! It's morbific, I tell you! *Ahhhh . . .*"

I heard the sound of barfage. It was Rosemary, doing the vocals of vomit.

"*G-u-huh-u-v-v-v-BLEAH!*"

You want to know how bad that smell was? It was so bad, I didn't even notice Rosemary's extrusion aroma.

"Let me out! Air! I need air!" Roy shouted. "This is worse than any poopfume! *Aiiir!*"

Suddenly it came to me. Something soft, yet crusty . . . something that smelled like it had crawled into a corner and died. . . .

"It's dirty socks!" I cried. "That's what it is! Socks!"

The light snapped on.

We all looked around. Hanging from each of us, like the ornaments on a Christmas tree, were socks. Black socks. Argyle socks. White socks. They hung from the paintings. They hung from the chandelier.

I looked up. The ceiling was high, like five times as high as most ceilings. But I could see the hidden door that had been used to pelt us with the reeking footwear.

The lawyer was standing by the light switch. Obviously he was the one who turned the lights back on.

He was wearing a gas mask.

Roy had a wild look in his little brown piggy eyes. His beefy shoulders and wide belly and thick neck were quivering from the gack dance as his stomach tried to blow.

I recognized the signs because my own guts were ready to hurl up a kidney. But I fought it. If Roy wasn't going to barf, I wasn't going to, either.

It was a matter of honor.

But the sight of Rosemary, dripping steaming hot gumbo down the front of her dress, didn't help.

"You are experiencing Elmont's sock collection," the lawyer said, like it made perfect sense. "There are one hundred and sixty pairs. He wore each pair for six months straight. Then he stored them, unwashed, in a closed bucket so that over the years the stench would grow and mature and intensify. It was a dream of his. You may say it was a crazy dream, but it was a dream just the same. To make a sock that could actually drive a person mad!"

"Yeah, well, it worked. I'm getting some air. Air! I'm gonna open that door and nobody better try and stop me," Tyler said. He bolted for the door we came in through.

Tyler's hand was on the knob when the lawyer spoke. "You are free to leave at any time. No one will dream of trying to stop you."

Tyler froze. I could see him struggling. He was fighting the terrible need for air. "I didn't say I was *leaving*."

"If so much as one hair of your head passes through the door, you are disqualified," the lawyer said. I couldn't tell if he was enjoying all this or not. It's kind of hard to tell if a guy is laughing when he's wearing a gas mask.

Slowly . . . slowly . . . Tyler stepped back from the door. But I could see his snooty face quivering and twitching. He took the end of his tie . . . yes, he was actually wearing a tie! What can I tell you? The boy thinks he's going to be president someday. Anyway, Tyler took the end of his tie and stuffed it in his mouth to try and hold back the wave of hurl that threatened to go airborne at any moment.

"It'f going to kake more van sock stench to get me to run," Tyler mumbled through his tie.

"I . . . can't . . . hold . . . my . . . breath . . . any . . . MORE!" Annette gasped.

I had totally forgotten Annette! And she was my responsibility.

"Look, you have to breathe," I told her. "You just have to accept it. Be brave."

She exhaled. She breathed in.

Then she grinned and promptly fainted. I grabbed her so she wouldn't hit the floor. I lifted her tiny limp body in my arms.

"Do you all know what this means?" I shouted.

They all stopped and stared at me.

"It means that even though he's dead, Uncle Elmont is trying to gross us out the door!"

EIGHT

"Air! Sweet, pure air!"

The lawyer finally let us out of that cursed entryway. We piled through the door into the next room, more dead than alive.

Annette began to revive. My stomach returned to its normal place.

We were in this huge room with two massive wooden staircases. One led left, the other right.

"I can almost smell the supernaturalness of this place," Sondra said.

"I don't think I'll ever be able to smell anything, ever, as long as I live," I said. "My nose is burned out."

"Do you really think that those socks were natural?" Sondra demanded. "Don't you realize they

45

were materialized by Uncle Elmont's ghost?"

"Sondra, there was a trapdoor in the ceiling. I saw it. That's how the socks appeared. Uncle Elmont obviously set it all up before he died."

"You can believe whatever you want to believe," Sondra said. "But I still say: Nothing natural could have smelled that heinous."

"You may each go up to your rooms now," the lawyer said.

"Our rooms?" Roy was suspicious. I couldn't blame him.

"A room has been assigned to each of you," the lawyer said. "At the top of the stairs."

"Yeah, right," I said. "Like we're going to trust you? No offense, but I think this whole thing is kind of a trap."

"And yet the door is always unlocked and you can leave at any time."

"Yeah, Sethie, you can leave anytime you want," Roy sneered. "I'll be happy to take your part of the money."

"Hey, we *all* split whatever is left after one of us leaves," Rosemary said. Rosemary is around nine, and she looks like this sweet girl. She dresses kind of old-fashioned and wears her hair in these long blond pigtails. But I guess she has a greedy streak like anyone.

"I won't be the first one to bail out," I said. "You forget something: I was always Uncle Elmont's favorite. He tortured me with more grossness than the rest of you ever had to deal with. So I'm prepared. I'm tough. I can handle it."

Roy grinned a mean grin. "Oh, yeah? Then you can go up the stairs first."

"You sure walked right into that," Annette said in disgust.

She was right. I had just talked my way into going first.

I turned to the lawyer. He was taking off his gas mask. It tugged at his hair, and he had a hard time getting it off. But he was looking at me with amusement. And it was weird, because I suddenly noticed something: He had one brown eye and one blue eye.

At least that's how it looked. It was hard to tell in the gloominess of that house. I shook it off. I mean, if he really had two different color eyes I would have noticed when we were all at the lawyer's office, right? That's not the kind of thing you overlook.

"So," I said to the lawyer, "which stairway do I take?"

He shrugged.

"I mean, where are the rooms? Left or right?"

He shrugged again.

It was getting so I really didn't like that guy.

I looked at the left stairway. It looked okay. Then I looked at the right-hand stairway. It looked okay, too. It was impossible to tell which led where. But I had this bad feeling that if I chose the wrong stairway, I would get to the top and something gross would be waiting for me.

Or maybe it didn't matter which one I chose.

"I feel good about the left," I announced. "Let's try it."

Tyler shook his head. "No, you try it."

"Me? Alone?"

"Not chicken, are you, Sethie?" Roy asked.

The answer was yes. But of course I said, "Why would I be afraid? Being down here with you is gross enough. How much worse could anything be?"

Roy isn't a guy who likes to be teased. He balled up his fists and started to come after me.

But Rosemary grabbed Roy's arm. "If you pound him, he can't go up those stairs and see what's up there," she said.

Roy thought about that for a moment. A moment is all the time he ever spends thinking. "Yeah, Sethie, go ahead. Climb the stairs. See what's waiting for us up there."

"The spirit of Uncle Elmont," Sondra said. "I can feel his presence."

"Oh, shut up, Sondra," I muttered.

I started toward the stairs. Annette was right. I had walked right into a stupid trap. Now I could either refuse to go and let Roy pound me, or I could go ahead and run into whatever was waiting for me up there.

I placed my foot on the first step. It seemed like a normal stair.

I took another step. Another. Another.

I was starting to feel a little better. Maybe I had misjudged. Maybe Uncle Elmont was done torturing us.

Yeah, right.

Another step. Another.

My mind went back to an earlier time when Uncle Elmont had tricked me into thinking he was going to leave me alone.

Flashback . . . flashback . . . flashback . . .

It was on my birthday. Just last year.

Uncle Elmont said he wanted to be there. He invited us to have the party here, at this house. Naturally I refused. Instead we all went out to a restaurant because we figured, What could go wrong in a restaurant?

49

I climbed another step, remembering that day.

It had started with the cake. Normally with Uncle Elmont around I would have checked that cake ten different ways before I cut into it. But it was in a restaurant. The restaurant made the cake. It was impossible for Uncle Elmont to mess with the cake.

Impossible!

Only not completely impossible. See, like I said, Uncle Elmont was rich. Very, very rich. So when I refused to have my party at his house and went to the restaurant instead, he *bought* the restaurant.

Too bad I didn't know that at the time.

What happened when I cut into the cake? . . . Nothing. See, I was too distracted to pay attention. I was smiling while my dad took videos. So I cut myself a great big piece and another piece for someone else. Then my mom took over the cutting.

I like cake. So I loaded one big, huge mound of cake on my fork. It was white cake. White frosting and white cake and little, tiny, white things wiggling and squirming and crawling.

Maggots!

My birthday cake was crawling with maggots!

NINE

I popped the cake in my mouth.

Then my mom said, "OH! OH! OH! Oh, *nooooo*! *Nooo!*" She was pointing at the cake in total, complete horror.

This was my first clue that something was wrong.

My second clue was that the cake in my mouth was *moving!*

Food that is still moving as you chew it is not a good thing.

"*Y-yaa-AAH!*"

I spewed the maggoty cake clear across the table. It hit Sondra right in the mouth.

But spitting it out wasn't enough. Because I could look down at my lump of half-chewed spitty cake and see the little things crawling and squirming.

And worse, much worse, I could feel some of them still crawling and squirming between my cheeks and my gums.

There was no waiting. No warning. No gack dance.

"Ugh-uugh-ugh-bub-b-b-buh-BLEAAAH!"

I blew chunks with such force that they broke the sound barrier. Some of my chunks hit the wall several yards away.

"Guuv-v-v-BLEAH!"

I barfed up food from two days before. I heaved a load so massive, it was like a stinking yellow Niagara Falls. I mean, I was gacking up my intestines.

Naturally Sondra, with her own mouth covered with my spewed maggot cake, extruded, too. Her extrusion hit me full in the face.

This set off universal hufferage.

Not only were all my friends heaving. Not only were my parents yodeling with their mouths full of gumbo. Everyone else in the restaurant was bubbling over with used food, barfing and hurling and chucking till the tables overflowed with steaming stomach soup.

"Ha-HA!" Uncle Elmont laughed so hard, he spit out his false teeth. They went cartwheeling across the table, trailing slobber.

And when it was all over, when the entire restaurant was a shallow lake of vomit, I figured, well, he really got me good.

But what I didn't think was: There's going to be *more*.

Now, as I climbed the last few steps up that stairway, I reminded myself—the death snot, the fartwater, even the socks of doom, they weren't the end. Uncle Elmont still had more planned.

He *always* had more planned.

I reached the top of the stairs. There was a hallway right before me. I saw doors. On the doors were names. "Rosemary" was on one, "Roy" on another, and so on.

I looked down at the others. The only one I cared about was Annette. And to be honest, I didn't care all that much about her. But at least I had shown everyone I was no chicken.

"It looks good," I said. "It's safe to come up this far."

"Says *you*," Roy sneered.

"You chicken, Roy?" I said. I was scared of Roy, but you know how it is when you're a guy—you can't ever act scared. And the way to not act scared is to be a complete idiot and say something dumb. "I did it, Roy, but I guess I'm just a little tougher than you think."

Annette was the first one to start up the stairs.

Roy sort of growled. Then he took the stairs two at a time. Everybody else followed him.

It was when they were almost at the top of the stairs that it happened.

SHHWAPP!

The stairs suddenly went smooth. I don't know how else to explain it. All at once they weren't stairs at all. They were just this long, smooth slope.

A long, smooth, *slippery* wood slope.

There was a horrible frozen moment when they all just stood there. They weren't standing on stairs anymore.

I saw Roy's legs start running. It was like a cartoon. You know, like when Wile E. Coyote runs off the side of a cliff and he's still running, only there's no ground under his feet?

The five of them—Roy, Annette, Sondra, Tyler, and Rosemary— slipped. The five of them fell on their stomachs. The five of them began sliding like sleds toward the bottom!

Fortunately they wouldn't be hurt. It wasn't

like they were going to run into something hard at the bottom of the stairs. No, what waited for them down there was soft.

Soft as cotton.

See, when the stairs suddenly flattened out, a wide trapdoor opened at the bottom of the stairs.

The door opened on a mass of white and orange. I had to squint to be sure it was what it looked like.

I was sorry I squinted. Because it was *exactly* what it looked like. Thousands . . . no, *millions* of Q-Tips.

Millions of the tiny white swabs. And on the end of each was a big gooey glob of orange.

Earwax!

I recoiled in shock and dismay.

My cousins . . . my sister . . . they were plunging toward the greatest collection of ear-wax the world had ever known!

"*Aaaaaaaaaaaaaahh!*" they screamed.

TEN

"Help!" Annette cried as she skidded down toward the earwax. "Seth, save me!"

Is there any brother with a heart so cold that he wouldn't respond at such a moment? Wouldn't you try and save your brother or sister from slithering into a jumble of a million earwax-dripping Q-Tips?

"Seth! I can't stop!"

I grabbed the nearest railing. I leaned down as far as I could. Annette's little hand stretched up toward me.

I touched her fingers. But then she slipped another six inches.

I had to think fast. I whipped off my belt and tossed the buckle end of it to Annette.

She caught it!

Slowly I began to draw her toward me.

But there was nothing I could do for the others. They were doomed.

"*Nooooo!*" Rosemary screamed. She was the lowest one. She was scrabbling, trying to hold on, but it was no good. Her feet hit the Q-Tips and made a crunchy sound.

She managed to pull one foot back out. She stared at it in horror. It bristled with sticky Q-Tips. They stuck out of her like a porcupine's quills. Then she fell facedown.

The earwax acted like glue. Q-Tips covered her. The more she struggled, the more the orange ingredient stuck to her.

"You!" Roy screamed up at me. "You did this! You said it was safe!"

"I . . . I . . ."

But there wasn't much point in discussing things with Roy. He slid helplessly into that horrible mass of cotton and ear goo.

Roy struggled, but the more he struggled, the deeper he went.

Roy surfaced, howling. "I'll KIIILL you, Seth!" But there were orange earwax probes sticking out of his tongue!

Then Tyler slid into him and down they both went.

I guess that did it for Tyler. He swam—I mean, I guess you'd call it swimming. Kind of. He worked his way to the far side of the deadly wax pit and climbed out.

He ran for the door. "Let me out of this insane asylum!"

Sondra was the last one to take the dive. She fought it down to the very end, but at the last minute, once it was clear she couldn't win, she just folded her hands and said, "I surrender myself to the mystic forces of karma."

I thought that was kind of cool.

But after she sank into the waxy mess she popped back up screaming, "Ugh! Ugh! NO! It's too horrible!"

So I guess her coolness didn't last.

We could still hear Tyler. We heard him open the front door. We heard him yammering like a ninny about showers and baths and how he was glad Uncle Elmont was dead!

Then something really terrible happened.

SWAPP!

The stairs suddenly snapped back to normal.

I stared down at my three cousins standing waist deep in used Q-Tips. They were totally earwaxed.

They stared up at me and Annette, both waxless.

"I think we better get out of here," I whispered to Annette.

"I think you're right," she agreed.

"GET HIM!" Roy screamed.

Up they climbed, emerging from the pit like dinosaurs that weren't quite ready to be swallowed by the lava.

"Run!" I yelled.

"Don't let them get away!" Rosemary yelled, her face decorated with a thousand orange globs.

"They must both suffer earwaxing!" Sondra cried.

I grabbed Annette's hand and took off down the hall at a high rate of speed.

"There!" Annette yelled.

She was pointing at the door with my name on it. I opened the door. I pushed Annette inside. I jumped in after her. I slammed the door behind me just as three very angry people slammed into it.

I threw the lock.

"Come out here and face your karma!" Sondra yelled.

"Come out here and face my fist!" Roy shouted.

They pounded for a while as Annette and I cowered inside. But I guess someone figured out that there were bathrooms in each of the rooms. Bathrooms with showers.

I think they all really, really wanted to take showers. Although I don't know what kind of soap it would take to remove the deadly orange goo pimples.

"I think they're gone," Annette said. She had been sitting with her ear pressed against the door.

"I don't care. I am never leaving this room," I said. I looked at my watch. "We only have twenty-three and a half hours left."

"We're going to spend twenty-three and a half hours in here with no food and no TV and no books to read?" Annette wailed.

"Would you rather go out and try and convince Roy and the others that it wasn't our fault what happened to them?"

Annette considered that for a moment. "I guess this room is okay."

"This room is our home for the next twenty-three hours, and nothing . . . *nothing* is going to get me to leave."

What on earth makes me say stupid things like that?

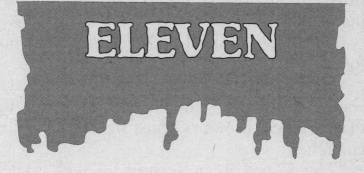

ELEVEN

"How much time do we have left now?" Annette asked.

I looked at my watch. Again. I had checked my watch approximately eight billion times. "We have fourteen hours left, give or take a few minutes."

"Fourteen hours. So we've been here ten hours."

"Ten hours, right."

"I'm hungry."

"I'm hungry, too."

"I'm *starving*."

"I'm starving, too."

"We have to go find some food."

It wasn't a bad room we were in. I mean, it looked a little like something from an old

Munsters rerun, with these big carved wood beds and the usual paintings of unhappy-looking people.

But there was no TV. No games. And no food.

"Maybe there's nothing more to worry about," Annette said hopefully. "I mean, maybe Uncle Elmont's ghost figures it's done enough."

"This is not about a ghost," I said. "This was all planned by Uncle Elmont before he died. He worked it all out and hired that creepy lawyer guy to trap us in here."

"I guess Uncle Elmont is up in heaven laughing at all this," Annette said.

"*Heaven?*" I repeated. "I don't think so. I'm thinking someplace warmer. But don't ever start believing he's finished with us. Uncle Elmont always has some new trick, some new way to make us miserable. Don't forget my birthday. I thought the maggot cake was all there was. Remember what happened next?"

"Like I could ever forget?"

"My present was supposed to be a puppy!" I wailed as the horrible memory came rushing back. "A puppy! It was a rat with some fake fur glued on!"

"Yeah, but Mom and Dad did buy you a real puppy—Ranger. I mean, once you gave the rat back to Uncle Elmont and all."

"A rat," I muttered. "He gave me a rat. He put maggots in my cake. He filled my myrrh with poodle poop and stuck a siren in my turban. And there are a hundred other times he's gotten me. Not even counting today. Why won't he leave me alone? Even now that he's dead, he's still torturing me with his sick practical jokes. And I'm the only member of the family who liked him even a little."

"Maybe Sondra is right," Annette suggested. "Maybe it's his ghost that's doing it all."

"Who knows," I admitted. "Maybe it is. All I know is I'm not leaving this room till tomorrow morning."

At that very moment the door swung slowly open.

I jumped up. "The door!"

"How did that happen?"

"How does anything happen in this place?" I moaned. I pushed the door shut. But it wouldn't catch. The lock just spun around when I tried to turn it.

"See what I mean?" I asked Annette bitterly.

"Uncle Elmont is never done. Never! He's the Energizer Bunny of practical jokers."

"At least now we can go out and look for food," Annette grumbled. "It's like dinnertime now. We totally missed lunch."

I hesitated. I could try and hide in the room. But what was the point? The lock had stopped working for a reason. Uncle Elmont had foreseen something like this. And he'd made some plan to keep me from being able to hide out.

Uncle Elmont wanted us out of our room. I had the feeling that one way or the other, we would have to go.

"Come on," I said. "Let's go find something to eat."

I opened the door and flinched. I expected . . . I don't know what I expected. Maybe Roy's fist in my face. Maybe some new trick from Uncle Elmont.

But what I saw was not Roy. It was the lawyer. I gave him a dirty look. He didn't care.

"Dinner will be served in the main dining room downstairs," he said.

"Down the stairs, huh? Yeah, right. Like I'm going to go down those stairs."

"I understand your skepticism. However, I

can tell you categorically that Uncle Elmont has no other . . . entertainments . . . planned."

"Ha! Uncle Elmont *always* has something else planned!"

"I assure you, young man, that is not the case. I swear, on my honor as an attorney, that he has no further tricks planned."

The strange thing was, he seemed to be telling the truth. I tried to look into his eyes and see if he was lying. Then I realized something.

"Hey, didn't you have one brown eye and one blue eye before?"

He seemed alarmed. "What? No, no, of course not! What a foolish question."

"I guess I was confused," I said thoughtfully. Why would he lie about something like that? It didn't make sense. I must have made a mistake.

"Dinner is being served downstairs. The others are already waiting. They have been told that they may not eat until you two arrive."

"Oh, great!" I said. "Now they hate me even more for making them wait. Come on, Annette."

I ran to the stairs. But I stopped at the top. I

looked back at the lawyer. "You swear? No more tricks?"

"I swear that *Elmont* has no more tricks planned."

I took a deep breath. I had no choice. I started down the stairs at a run. I reached the bottom safe and sound.

Maybe, just maybe, I thought, the lawyer is telling the truth.

And you know what's funny? He was. Kind of.

TWELVE

"There he is!" Sondra hissed.

"Get him!" Roy cried.

"Destroy him," Rosemary said.

The three of them were sitting at a table that was about as long as a basketball court.

At least they were sitting when Annette and I first walked into the room. As soon as they saw us they all jumped up.

Roy grabbed a fork off the table and started toward me.

"Now, now," the lawyer said. "None of that. We'll have no violence in my house." And with that he turned and went through the door that connected the dining room to the kitchen.

But Roy was still coming toward me with a

fork. I guess I should have been grateful there weren't any knives around.

"L-L-look, Roy," I stammered. "I—I—I didn't know about those stairs. I swear!"

It was Rosemary who answered. "Yeah, so how come we all end up scraping earwax off our skin while you and your sister get away clean?"

I looked to Sondra for help. "Probably some karma thing," I suggested.

"Blow it out your ear, Seth," Sondra sneered. "Uncle Elmont's ghost is working through you. He's using you to destroy us and force us all to run so we won't get any of the money!"

I've been accused of lots of things. But I've never been accused of being an accomplice of a ghost.

"Yeah, and we noticed something else," Rosemary said. "We're all the only kids in our families. So we can only get one share, and we only have one chance to survive. But there are two of you. *Two* shares. Two chances to survive."

I hadn't thought about that. I could see where they would be a little suspicious.

"I'm gonna pound you real good," Roy said.

But just then the lawyer returned. He was carrying a big tray of food.

"Young man," he snapped at Roy. "I said there will be no violence in Elmont's house. And I meant it. Any violence will disqualify you. It will be the same as if you left. You will lose your share."

Roy looked stunned. "That's not fair! Violence is all I got!"

"Dinner is served," the lawyer said.

"Like we'd ever eat any food in this house," Rosemary said. "We're not idiots."

"As you wish," the lawyer said. He laid out big steaming dishes of soup and vegetables, a big roast, and even a pie.

The five of us stared. We were all starving.

"I think maybe the food is okay," Sondra said. "I mean, I came down and looked around while it was cooking. It looked normal. So we could all eat, probably."

"I have an idea," Rosemary said, giving me the evil eye. "Let's have Seth taste everything first."

"Yeah," Roy agreed. "Yeah, let Sethie eat it."

"The lawyer told me there would be no more tricks," I said.

"Fine. Prove it," Sondra said. She pointed at the food. "Eat."

It didn't look like I had much of a choice. What was the worst that could happen?

I didn't want to think about the worst that could happen.

I piled my plate with a little of everything. I filled a bowl with soup. I grabbed a big wad of mashed potatoes. I even had some other vegetables. I sliced a big hunk of the roast.

Four sets of eyes watched me as I ate. Annette was also waiting to see what would happen. I just smiled and chewed.

"Hey, he's eating it," Roy said, pointing out the obvious.

"It must be okay—nothing's happened yet," Rosemary said.

"I'm starving!" Roy said. He started piling up his plate.

For the next ten minutes we just scarfed. We were all dying of hunger. And the food was tasty, especially the meat. It had an unusual flavor I hadn't experienced before. Could it be veal? I'd heard about veal, but I'd never had any.

"Anyone want the rest of those green beans?" Sondra asked. "I don't eat meat, so I have to fill up on the soup and the veggies."

"It's all yours," Roy said. "I like meat. It makes you strong. In fact, I'm gonna have some more."

He leaned across the table and started slicing away at the meat, cutting big, dripping hunks. But then the knife seemed to catch.

Roy frowned and pressed down harder. "Must be a bone or something," he said. He frowned harder. "No, wait, there's something here. . . ."

We all froze. Suddenly we all had the same terrible feeling of doom.

Roy struggled with the meat. Something appeared, something blue. Roy grabbed it and pulled.

Out it came. It was an inch thick. Blue nylon. A foot long. With a buckle.

Roy held it up to the light. "What on . . . what is it?"

"It looks like . . . like a collar. Like a DOG collar!" Rosemary wailed.

There was a little metal disk hanging from the buckle. Roy wiped the juices off it and read: "Ranger."

RANGER!

The horror hit me like a fist.

I had just eaten my own dog!

THIRTEEN

"You made us eat your dog!" Roy screamed. "I'm gonna pound you so bad—"

But I wasn't worried about Roy. I was horrified and upset and really, really sick.

My throat began to do the gack dance.

My stomach rented a trailer and moved to my throat.

The countdown began. The countdown to total, massive magoo!

"Bubub-GARGH-guv-v-BLEAAH!"

I heaved. I hurled. I did the blew magoo.

"SQUIRT!"

My guttal explosion sprayed like a fire hose. It hit Rosemary. The force of it knocked her back in her chair.

I was in total Pukatoa mode. I was barfacious to the tenth power.

I turned the force of the vomit cannon away from Rosemary and, unfortunately, hit Roy.

But Roy had also magooed. My gumbo hit his in midair. It was a midair gumbo collision.

"*SPLOOSH!*"

Both of us recoiled from the force. Stomach contents sloshed across the table, like a high tide coming in over the beach.

Rosemary tried to run from the tidal wave. She tried to escape the gutsunami. But too late! The rolling surf of stomach contents knocked her down again.

Then I noticed Sondra. She was untouched by the barfsplosion. She was cowering in a corner, out of the line of fire. She almost seemed to be smiling. Of course she, being a vegetarian, had not consumed any canine.

I also saw the lawyer's face. He looked surprised. His forehead was creased in thought.

But mostly I noticed Rosemary. She rose from beneath the table, where she had slipped after the vomit wave had rolled over her.

"*Ahhhhrrrrgggh!* I ate DOG! I'm covered in regrettable fluids!" Rosemary screamed. "I've been vomitized!"

And what made the screaming all the more upsetting was the fact that she was magooing even while she spoke. This was beyond just being the vocals of vomit. This was total vomitspeak! It was a whole new language: She was speaking vomish!

It was like, "I'm (*bleah!*) covered in (*ugh-bubluh*) regret (*phut-bleah!*)-table fluids!"

It was kind of funny, actually.

"I just can't take anymore!" And with that, Rosemary ran screaming from the room. *"Aaaaaa (bleah!) arrrrrg-g-g-ghhhh (blech!)"*

We could hear her screaming and hurling all the way down the hall.

We heard the sound of a door slamming. Only then did the screaming stop. Although I later found out she went on screaming until the following Tuesday.

I felt something tugging on my sleeve. It was Annette. She had been hit pretty bad in the vomit storm. But she didn't look nearly as upset as I felt.

"We better get out of here," she whispered. "There's something I have to tell you!"

I decided she was right. Staying there with Roy and Sondra didn't seem like a good idea. I backed toward the hallway. As soon as we were out of the room we ran back up to our bedroom.

I slammed the door shut behind me. It still wouldn't lock.

Then it hit me. "Ranger! I ate Ranger!"

"That's what I wanted to tell you," Annette said. "No way was that Ranger."

"What do you mean?"

"Seth, think about it. How big is Ranger? I mean, if you took away his head and fur and tail, how much meat would you actually have?"

I had to think about that. But I didn't have to think for very long. "You'd have, like, I don't know, like one pound. He's small and he's skinny."

"And that meat downstairs was big. Way too big to be Ranger."

"It was a trick!" I cried. I slammed my fist into my palm. "Another of Uncle Elmont's tricks! He just baked Ranger's collar inside the meat so we would find it and think . . . hey. Wait a minute. I took Ranger for a walk just yesterday down to the park and he had his collar then. Did he have his collar this morning? I don't remember."

"I don't either," Annette admitted.

"So if Ranger had his collar for sure yester-

78

day, and Uncle Elmont's been dead for a week, how did Uncle Elmont get Ranger's collar?"

"Maybe Sondra is right—he's a ghost. I guess ghosts can do anything they want to do. They're supernatural."

"Uncle Elmont is not a ghost," I said firmly. "But there is definitely *something* going on here. Something is not what it seems."

"So what do we do?"

"We go looking for an answer. And I think I know right where to start looking: Uncle Elmont's room."

"Do you even know where it is?"

"I think so. I saw a big door at the end of the hallway. You can wait here if you want."

"No way," Annette said. "But let's clean this barf off us first."

It took a while to clean up. Even then the gaggable aroma of guttal gumbo wafted around us.

I led the way back out into the hallway. We crept down the carpet toward Uncle Elmont's room.

"It'll probably be locked," I said. I put my hand on the doorknob and twisted. "It's not locked!" I whispered. I was excited and kind of scared.

I opened the door and stepped inside.

It was decorated the same way as most of the house. Lots of dark wood and gold-framed paintings.

My gaze was drawn to a huge, very ornate cupboard against the wall. It had all kinds of doors and drawers.

"Let's look in there."

"You first," Annette said.

I pulled open a drawer. Socks. I closed it real fast. They were clean, but I'd had enough of Uncle Elmont's socks to last a lifetime.

The next drawer was underwear. The next drawer was T-shirts.

"This is about as exciting as shopping at a department store," I muttered. "What's next? Pajamas?" I opened the last drawer. "Yep. Pajamas."

"Try one of those cupboards," Annette suggested. "Try opening that one." She pointed at the most ornate door in the cupboard.

"Okay. Here goes—"

"AAAAH!"

"AAAAH!"

"Teeth!"

"Gross!"

There, lined up in six glasses of water, were six sets of false teeth.

FOURTEEN

"E*eeewwww!*"

   "*Guh-ross!*"

Wham! I slammed the cabinet door shut.

But then something made me hesitate. "I have to look in there again."

"What? You want to look at all those teeth again? Uncle Elmont's used teeth?"

"You can look away," I said. "But sometimes a man's gotta do what a man's gotta do."

I steeled myself for the horrible sight. Then, slowly, I opened the cabinet. There they were: bright pink gums. Big white teeth. All grinning at me from their glasses. It was like some sort of insane aquarium.

But I'd been wrong the first time. Not six glasses with six sets of teeth. It was *seven*

81

glasses with *six* sets of false teeth.

"There are teeth missing!" I said.

"What? You want more?" Annette was covering her eyes.

"What are you two doing?"

We both jumped about three feet in the air and spun around.

"I asked what you two are doing here," Sondra repeated. She had snuck into the room behind us.

"What are we doing in here? Um . . . looking for something?"

Sondra gave me a sort of squinty look. "You were communicating with Uncle Elmont's ghost, weren't you?"

I rolled my eyes. "Sondra, you're being ridiculous. Uncle Elmont is dead. There's no such things as ghosts. And why would I want to help Uncle Elmont torture all of us?"

"To get rid of me and Roy. That way you and Annette get all of Uncle Elmont's money."

"You can believe whatever you want to believe," I said. "But you're nuts." I began to stomp out of the room with Annette right behind me. Then I saw something that made me stop suddenly.

It was a picture. Not one of the big gold-framed paintings. This was a color photograph of Uncle Elmont. He was just snickering. I was struck by his eyes. Bright, sparkling blue.

And there was something else. Near the photograph was a small bottle labeled Saline Solution.

I had a strange, uneasy feeling. Like I was missing something important. Like something obvious was staring me in the face, but I just couldn't figure it out.

Out in the hallway I looked at Annette. We've never been all that close. I guess I always just thought of her as a typical dumb little sister.

But it was Annette who had figured out about the meat not being Ranger. And she'd been pretty tough so far. I decided to trust her.

"Something is going on here," I said. "I mean, something more than just Uncle Elmont doing practical jokes from beyond the grave."

Annette looked up at me with serious eyes. "Yes, but *what* is going on?"

"That's the mystery we have to solve," I said as we got to my room.

"We?" she asked.

"Yes. You and I have to stick together."

She took my hand and held it. She looked

up at me with adoring little-sister eyes and said, "Okay, but if you get pounded by Roy, you can do that part without me."

I suddenly felt tired. Fear and barfing will wear you out. In my room there were two big old-fashioned beds. They had huge carved wood posts and even had canopies. You know, those tentlike deals you see in movies about old-fashioned knights and all.

"We should take a rest and try to figure this all out," I said wearily. I went to the bed. I turned around and flopped straight back on the mattress.

WHAM!

The legs of the bed collapsed and the mattress hit the floor.

CREEAAK!

The four heavy posts began to tilt in.

THUD! THUD! THUD! THUD!

One by one the posts landed on me. As they fell they brought the canopy down, too. I was trapped under a sheet of satin, held down by massive wooden poles.

"Seth!" Annette screamed. She started pulling the bedposts off me.

I slithered out from under the canopy and straightened my shirt, which had gotten wrapped around me.

"Are you hurt?" Annette asked.

"Ha! No, I'm not hurt." I was grinning like an idiot. "I'm not hurt at all."

"You could have been, though," Annette said angrily. "Uncle Elmont is going too far now!"

"Uncle Elmont?" I repeated, arching my brow. "I don't think so, Annette. I don't know *who* sawed through the bed legs and the posts, but it sure wasn't Uncle Elmont or even Uncle Elmont's ghost."

"How can you be sure?"

"What is the one thing every single one of Uncle Elmont's practical jokes always involves?" I answered my own question. "*Grossness*. Grossness is the key! And this little prank was annoying and cruel, but it was not gross. It was not Uncle Elmont!"

"You mean . . ."

"Yes. The single-joker theory is wrong! There is a second practical joker! And his name is *Roy!*" I balled my hands up into fists. "That does it! Maybe I can't do anything about Uncle Elmont, but I've lived in fear of Roy for too long. I don't care if he is bigger than me. And stronger than me. And meaner than me. I'm going to get him good! I'm going to find a way to force him out of this house so he'll lose his share of Uncle Elmont's money!"

Annette looked at me skeptically. "Really? He'll pound you."

"I'm not afraid anymore," I said.

"Really?"

"Um . . . no. No, I'm not afraid."

"Okay."

"But I am sleepy. And before I can get my revenge on Roy and destroy him, I'm just going to take a little nap." I began clearing away my bed. "I'll destroy him better if I rest first."

Okay, fine, I know what you're thinking. You're thinking I chickened out. That I was still afraid of Roy pounding me.

All right, so I was afraid. But it just so happens, if you'll keep reading, you'll see it all worked out for the best.

So there.

I fell asleep thinking of ways to get Roy back. Ways that would not involve me ending up pounded.

When I awoke at last, I awoke to the ultimate nightmare. A horror beyond my wildest imagining!

FIFTEEN

I dreamed.

In my dream I was being chased by a gigantic Q-Tip dripping orange ear goo. I ran and ran to escape the earwax devil, but then ahead of me I saw Ranger. He was wearing socks. And he appeared to be standing in a frying pan.

He was simmering in regrettable fluids.

I screamed in my sleep.

Suddenly I was face-to-face with Uncle Elmont. He was sitting in the lawyer's chair at the office. He was asking me where my myrrh was.

"I don't know!" I wailed.

Uncle Elmont laughed and laughed until one of his eyes turned brown.

Then I was back at home. Only Sondra was there, too. She was saying we should all stick together. She was petting Ranger and asking him how he tasted.

And Ranger said, "Ha-HA!"

When I looked away from Ranger, I realized I was surrounded. Surrounded by chattering teeth. Huge, huge false teeth. Millions of them.

I woke up screaming. *"Aaaaaahhhhhhh! Aaaahhhhh!"*

"Ooooohhhh! Oooooohhhhh!"

Someone else was screaming too!

The room was pitch dark. I felt a shiver go up my spine, a cold draft. Was I really awake? Yes! I was awake.

If only I had been asleep! If only I didn't have to face the unspeakable horror!

It took me a second to notice it. Then I realized . . . something was wrong with my mouth!

Something was TERRIBLY WRONG WITH MY MOUTH!

I could barely move my lips. Something had happened. I touched it. I put my hand to my mouth.

"AAAAAAHHHHHHH!" Now I really screamed.

Something was in my mouth!

I scrambled for the light switch. I missed and knocked over a lamp.

"OOOOOHHHHHH!"

I recognized the voice of the other screamer. It was Annette.

I reached the wall switch. I snapped on the lights.

Right in front of me was Annette. Her entire mouth was . . . it was . . . her teeth . . . her gums . . . !

"AAAAAAHHHHHH!"

"OOOOOOHHHHHHH!"

I ran for the mirror. What I saw made my insides turn to liquid. My knees turned to jelly.

I had huge, huge bright pink gums.

I had big horsey teeth.

My big gums and big teeth were so big that my lips were drawn way back to make room. I had the grin of a skeleton.

A skeleton with really large gums.

It was not a pretty sight.

Then, slowly, the realization dawned on me. Dread washed over me. Terror and sickness filled me. It was the worst thing imaginable! It was the unspeakable evil!

I had Uncle Elmont's false teeth glued into my own mouth with Poli-Grip!

"AAAAAAAHHHHHHH!"

Annette had another pair glued into *her* mouth.

"OOOOOOHHHHHH!"

And they would NOT come out!

I leapt for the door. I'd had enough. I'd had *more* than enough.

Out the bedroom door!

"AAAAAAAHHHHHHH!"

"OOOOOOOHHHHHHH!"

Down the hall! We ran! We ran and ran, screaming like lunatics.

BAM!

Something slammed into me. It knocked me down. I was up in a flash.

ROY!

I stared into his wild eyes. I stared at his mouth!

Roy had dentures, too.

He looked at me and screamed, "UUUU-URRRRRGGGGHHH!"

I looked at him and screamed, "AAAAAAAHHHHHH!"

Annette looked at both of us and screamed, "OOOOOHHHHH!"

The three of us pelted down the stairs two steps at a time.

Uncle Elmont's teeth were in my mouth! Uncle Elmont's old, slimy, fake gums were glued into my mouth!

I had an elderly dead man's slobber on me!

Death slobber!

I couldn't control my stomach. My stomach really didn't like the idea of someone else's gums in my mouth.

I did a running magoo. I served up stomach contents as I ran. Flying gut gumbo streamed out of both sides of my mouth.

"BLEAAH!"

It was full-speed vomit!

Roy blew next. He hurled as he hurtled down the stairs.

Just like Rosemary, we ran screaming and gacking, yammering and heaving, babbling and blowing chunks of steamy stomach contents.

It was not a dignified retreat. It was all-out panic puking.

The three of us reached the front door of the house. In two seconds we would be out, through that door, away from Uncle Elmont's insane house.

In two seconds we would lose all the money.

I reached for the door handle.

I turned it.

SIXTEEN

The door opened.

Fresh air wafted in. Out in the driveway the parental cars were parked. The parents themselves were sleeping in the seats.

Those cars represented everything I wanted right then: a normal world. My own room. TV.

Then, just an inch from crossing the threshold, I froze.

"Hey, wheref Honra?" I asked.

Roy tried to shove me aside and get at the doorknob himself. But I grabbed his arms and looked into his face. Which was not an easy thing to do. Because even at the best of times Roy is not a great-looking guy. But in the middle of the night, with his hair sticking up and the front of his pajamas plastered with chunks of steaming hot gumbo and a big huge pair of dentures bursting out of his mouth . . . well, it was one of my worst nightmares.

"Roy! Wheref Honra!" I repeated. "Why ihn'k he here, hoo?"

Roy still didn't get it. But Annette did. "Honra! You're hrike!"

I slammed the door shut.

Translated, what I had said was, "Where's Sondra? Why isn't she here, too?" It's not easy to talk with extra teeth and gums in your mouth.

It took Roy a few more minutes. But at last he said, "Are you hayin he hig hihk?"

Translated from denture language, that meant, "Are you saying she did this?"

Annette and I both nodded.

Roy looked suspicious, but suddenly none of us was interested in opening the door and leaving.

I pointed in the direction of the kitchen. Roy looked doubtful, but then he nodded. I closed the door.

The three of us went to the kitchen, where I boiled water to make hot tea.

We sipped hot tea. Although given the extra teeth and gums, it wasn't exactly like when the queen of England has tea. It was more like three drooling, vomitacious hogs having tea. But the hot tea did start to work. It loosened the dentures.

We finished off by biting into apples. This broke the hold of the Poli-Grip.

I spit the dentures out of my mouth. They skittered across the table, leaving a trail of slobber and puke.

"Okay, now, what's going on?" Roy demanded. "Someone is going to get pounded. I just want to know who."

"Look," I said. "I have an idea, but I'm not totally sure. But first of all, Roy, you have to be totally honest with me."

"Totally honest?"

"I just have one question for you: Are you the one who sawed through the legs of my bed?"

He looked confused. "Huh? What are you talking about?"

"So. It wasn't you at all. It all fits together now," I said.

Roy shrugged and glared at me. "I don't even know what you're talking about."

"I'm talking about grossness, Roy. From the death snot at the funeral, to the fartwater at the lawyer's office, to the socks of doom, to the earwax hell pit, to the nightmare dentures, it was all gross. But sawing the legs of my bed was *not* gross. That's why it pointed straight to you, Roy."

He looked like he was trying to think. I think it was his first time. "But I didn't do it!"

I nodded. "Yes, I know that now. That was her big mistake!"

"Her? You mean Sondra?"

"Yes, Sondra," I sneered, "the *second* joker!"

"The second . . ."

"First there was Uncle Elmont. Uncle Elmont set up the trick with the socks and the trick with the earwax. And he arranged it so that my door wouldn't stay locked. But everything else was Sondra. It *had* to be Sondra who pulled the trick with Ranger. See, Roy, that was *not* Ranger we ate."

"It wasn't?"

"No. I realized that right away." I avoided looking at Annette. I think she rolled her eyes. But I didn't want to complicate the story by mentioning that it was actually her who figured out about Ranger.

"Sondra was over at my house yesterday morning," I said. "Supposedly she wanted us all to work together. In reality she was there to steal Ranger's collar. Then she planted it under the meat! That got rid of Rosemary."

"Then she sabotaged my bed. Why? So I would think it was you, Roy. She deliberately did something that was not like a typical Elmont trick so that I would suspect you."

"But why?" Roy wondered.

"To get rid of you, Roy," Annette said. "She figured Seth would be so mad, he'd go looking for you. Remember how the lawyer said if anyone was violent, they would be disqualified?"

Roy nodded. "Yeah. It was way unfair."

"And what would you have done if Seth had gotten mad and yelled at you for sawing the bed?"

"I would have pounded him," Roy said. I saw the light go on in his eyes as he figured it out. "Hey! Sondra wanted me to pound Seth because then I'd lose my share of the money!"

"But it didn't work because I was too smart," I said.

Annette looked at me with a raised eyebrow. "Uh-huh," she said. "Seth was too smart to go and get pounded."

"And when Annette and I investigated Uncle Elmont's bedroom and found his sets of false teeth, Sondra was there, too. She also kept talking about how it was Uncle Elmont's ghost doing all these tricks. Why? Because if we were afraid as well as grossed out, we'd be even more likely to give up."

Roy's little piggy eyes got narrow and mean.

"Sondra, huh? Why, I should . . . hey," he said in sudden confusion. "I can't pound Sondra. She's a girl."

I grinned. "No need to pound her, Roy. We're going to get Sondra! It's—" I checked my watch. "It's three o'clock in the morning. Five hours till the twenty-four hours is up. We have five hours! We are going to pay Sondra back."

SEVENTEEN

E asier said than done.

We knew we wanted to pay Sondra back good. But how? How?

"She'll be expecting us to try something," Annette pointed out.

"That's right," Roy agreed. "Hey! Maybe Annette could pound her. I mean, they're both girls, right? So it would be okay."

I rolled my eyes. Annette was eight years old and weighed less than fifty pounds. But then, Roy was not a guy who would be going on to college someday, if you know what I mean. In fact, I wasn't sure he'd make it into high school.

I looked around the kitchen, waiting for an inspiration. "What do we have to work with?"

Annette shrugged. "Food?"

I nodded. "Yes, food. Now, what would she eat? She's a vegetarian, remember. What do vegetarians eat for breakfast?"

The three of us frowned at each other.

"Granola!" we all said at once.

Roy ran to the cupboards and began flinging them open one after another. "Raisin Bran. Bran Flakes. Bran Buds. Tasty Bran. Boy, I guess Uncle Elmont liked bran. There! Granola!"

He snatched the box and handed it to me.

"Now what?" Annette asked.

I hesitated. I wasn't really sure what to do. "I . . . I . . . I don't know," I admitted helplessly.

"Me neither," Annette said.

"Uncle Elmont would sure know what to do," Roy muttered.

"That's it!" Annette snapped her fingers. "Seth, you are the only one in our entire family who ever thought anything Uncle Elmont did was funny."

"That's because I'm the only one with a sense of humor," I said.

"Exactly! You have to use that force, Seth. Let it flow through you. Use the force, Seth!"

I nodded slowly. She was making sense.

"You need to *become* Uncle Elmont," Annette said. "Get in touch with your inner Elmont."

"Yes! That's it!" I cried.

"Elmontize!" Annette cried enthusiastically. "It's our only hope. And only you can do it, Seth!"

"Okay. No one say anything! I have to concentrate. I have to embrace the Elmont that is deep within me!"

I sat down at the counter. I hung my head in my hands. I closed my eyes.

Uncle Elmont had always been a part of me, I realized. A gross, obnoxious part of me, sure, but a part just the same. I could see it now.

Suddenly, like a lightbulb going off in my head, I knew the answer! I knew how to gross Sondra out the door.

And then . . . there was a second lightbulb. All the clues fell into place. The vast, enormous scope of it all was clear to me. I had been raised to a mountaintop! I could see clearly now!

I raised my head. I rose to my feet. Annette and Roy looked at me, their eyes shining with hope.

"I know what we must do," I said firmly.

We worked like fiends for the next couple of hours. It took the rest of the night. It took teamwork. It took many strange ingredients.

And scariest of all, it required a terrifying spy mission into the very lair of the enemy!

But as the first rays of the sun shone through the windows of the big dining room, we were ready.

Oh, yes. We were ready for Sondra.

And for Uncle Elmont.

EIGHTEEN

"Here she comes!" Roy gasped breathlessly as he raced into the kitchen. "She's on the stairs!"

"Annette! Hit the microwave!" I rapped out the instruction like a sergeant.

Annette checked the pitcher of milk inside the microwave and hit the start button. We had experimented with the timing all night.

I threw open the freezer door and pulled out the bowl of granola. I raced into the dining room and set the bowl on the table.

Annette was right behind me with the milk.

The milk had to be just the right temperature. Not so warm that it steamed. Sondra would notice that, and the entire, careful plan would fail!

We raced back out of the dining room just as Sondra walked in.

The three of us stood with our ears pressed to the door. Waiting. Would she fall for it?

"Oh please, oh please, oh please," Annette whispered.

"Seth?" Sondra yelled.

My heart was in my throat.

"Seth? Annette? Roy?" she cried loudly.

For a frozen moment of time no one moved. Had Sondra guessed that we were still there?

Then we heard Sondra laugh. It was a wicked-sounding laugh. A laugh of triumph. "Ha!" she crowed. "So they did leave! I was right. The dentures did the trick. Ha, ha, that'll teach them to mess with me! I win!"

I cracked the door a fraction of an inch. Sondra was grinning like she'd just won the lottery. And I guess in a way she did. I mean, she thought Roy and Annette and I had bailed out last night. She thought we were gone, which meant that she, and she alone, inherited all of Uncle Elmont's money.

Like she was reading my mind, Sondra said, "All mine. Ha, ha, poor dumb losers. All of it *mine!*" She glanced at her watch. "Just another ten minutes! Just time enough for breakfast."

Then she sat down at the table and poured the milk over the granola.

She dipped in a spoon.

She raised the spoon to her mouth.

She chewed.

She swallowed.

The three of us practically burst out cheering. We gave each other silent high fives.

"A little more," I whispered. "She'll see it soon . . . any minute now . . ."

"What?" Sondra stared down at her bowl. But she stuck one last spoonful of granola into her mouth.

She stared a little harder at her granola. Like she couldn't quite believe what she was seeing.

Like she really, really didn't *want* to believe what she was seeing.

"BUGS!" she screamed.

She spit out the granola in her mouth. A half-chewed worm lay there in the mess of milk and cereal.

"WORMS!" she shrieked.

She jumped back from the table. Her chair scraped loudly.

"WORMS!" she cried again. "I've eaten worms!"

I peered closely at her throat. "We have

gack dance," I confirmed. "I'd say about ten seconds to massive magoo!"

I was wrong. It was only about three seconds.

"U-U-U-UGH-UGH-GU-GU-GUV-BLEAAH!"

"We have magoo," Annette whispered, sounding satisfied.

Sondra was shrieking and puking at the same time. Screaming and hurling, which makes a fairly awful sound.

And yet Sondra is not like Tyler or Rosemary. Sondra may be strange and rotten, but she has a core of inner strength.

Even as she cried and wailed and barfed all at once, she checked her watch.

"Ha! (*Bu-ubleah!*) Eight o' (*guv-bu-bleah!*) clock! I've (*hug-gug-bleah!*) made it!"

Still streaming puke, she ran from the dining room.

We waited a few seconds and went after her, careful to stay out of sight.

She reached the front door of the house. And Sondra being Sondra, checked her watch one last time.

Only then did she open the door.

She took one step outside. All the parents were camped out there in their cars.

"NOOOOOOOO!"

We could hear the sound of Sondra's mother screaming. "NOOOOO! You only had an hour to go! NOOOO!"

We stepped out of hiding. I was grinning so much my mouth hurt.

"It's five after eight!" Sondra wailed.

"Actually, Sondra," I said, "it's only five after *seven*."

She spun around and stared at me. "I—I thought you all left!"

"We almost did, Sondra," I said. "The denture trick almost did it. But we figured it out. And last night Annette snuck into your room. She took your watch from the nightstand and moved the time back one hour."

Sondra's face twitched. I think she was slightly angry.

"Would you like to know how we fixed your granola?" I offered. "It was very scientific. See, we collected roaches from under the refrigerator and termites from the walls and dug in the basement for worms. Then we added them to your granola. But we chilled the granola. Why? Because when they are very cold, bugs don't move much. And as long as they didn't move, we knew you'd never notice them in the granola. You can hide anything in granola."

Annette picked up the explanation. "Then we heated the milk. Just enough so that when the warm milk hit the cold granola, it would revive the bugs. It worked!"

"It worked," I repeated. "And now you, Sondra, are out. And we are in."

The three of us gave a little wave. I could see my parents outside, looking proud.

We shut the door on Sondra's angry cries.

"That was fun," Roy said. "Now we just have to hang out for an hour."

"Actually," I said, "there is one more little mystery to be dealt with."

NINETEEN

At eight o'clock the lawyer came down the stairs. We could hear him calling out, "Hello! Hello! Is anyone here?"

The three of us—me, my little sister, and Roy—hid ourselves in the broom closet of the kitchen.

"Hello? Hell-o-o-o? Anyone still here?"

The lawyer came through the dining room into the kitchen. We had cleaned the dining room of Sondra's bug barf and granola.

"Hello? Hey, anyone here? I guess not."

We heard him open the refrigerator door.

"Hello? Anyone who's here should come out now!"

We heard him close the refrigerator door.

Then, in a low voice, he muttered, "No one left. All gone. It worked. Ha-HA! It worked."

That's when I opened the broom closet door. "Not quite," I said.

He jumped about a foot straight up. He glared at us as we piled out. "You . . . you're still here?"

"That's right, Mr. *Lawyer*. Or should I say . . . *Uncle Elmont!*"

This time he jumped even higher. As a matter of fact, he was kind of jumpy for a very old dead person.

"What are you talking about?" he blustered.

"I'm talking about the fact that you are not a lawyer. You are Uncle Elmont."

"You're crazy," he protested.

"Oh, am I? I don't think so. I should have seen the clues earlier. I saw you with one brown eye and one blue eye. You're wearing colored contact lenses to make it look like you have brown eyes. But one of them must have slipped. Because one of your eyes was blue! Like Uncle Elmont's eyes. And then in your room we found saline solution! Saline solution is used by people who wear contact lenses!"

"That doesn't prove anything," he sneered.

"And then," I went on, "the other night at dinner, when you told Roy not to pound me, you said 'we'll have no violence in *my* house.'"

"That was just a slip of the tongue!" he said. But he was definitely nervous. He took a big drink of the apple juice he'd taken out of the refrigerator.

"Then there was the teeth. See, there were seven glasses, but only six pairs of dentures. *Someone* was wearing that seventh pair!"

"Maybe I—I mean, maybe Elmont was buried with a pair of dentures."

"Give it up, Uncle Elmont," Annette said pitilessly. "You lost."

"This was going to be your greatest practical joke," I said. "You would fake your own death. Then you would force us all to come here, where you could set up your deadly socks prank and your earwax pit of doom!"

He laughed sullenly. "You still don't even get the magnificence of it all," he said. He pulled the wig from his bald head. He was Uncle Elmont again. "I would fake my own death and then, after I had played my few tricks, I knew I could count on human nature to carry on!"

"What do you mean?" Roy asked.

"He means that his final trick was watching us turn against each other," I explained. "He knew that we would turn on each other. That one of

111

us, maybe more, would try to destroy the others and get all the money for themselves."

"And then, when all of you had failed the test, I would reappear and have a good laugh at your expense! Ha-HA!"

I smiled. "Too bad it didn't work, Uncle. Because, see, the three of us *did* survive. The three of us lasted all the way through. And now you have to split your money between us!"

Uncle Elmont just stood there, sputtering in anger. I guess I can understand how he felt. His greatest-ever practical joke had been foiled. We had beaten him.

But I realized something. I had beaten him, all right. But I had beaten him the only way I could—by accepting my own inner Elmont-hood. By *becoming* him.

I think there's some kind of irony there. Maybe.

It was definitely eight o'clock now. We had made it for the full twenty-four hours.

"Let's go," I said to Roy and Annette. I gave Roy a nudge, reminding him what he was supposed to say.

"Oh . . . um . . . hey, before we go, I gotta pee."

"Again?" I asked him. "You just peed a little while ago. In fact, we all did. . . ." I grinned up at Uncle Elmont. "You remember, Roy, when we whizzed in the apple juice!"

See, I had remembered Uncle Elmont from the video saying he drank nothing but apple juice in the morning.

It was a very satisfying thing, walking away as Uncle Elmont gagged and barfed and did the blew magoo. He blew his teeth—the missing seventh set of teeth—right out like a boulder blowing from Pukatoa.

Of course, we hadn't really done anything to his apple juice. But he didn't know that.

"I'll get (*huh-BLEAH*) you for (*bleah*) this!" Uncle Elmont cried in fluent vomitspeak as the three of us walked out to the welcoming arms of our loving families.

TWENTY

U ncle Elmont's mansion was just a fading memory when I woke up in my new king-size bed. The bed had comic sheets personally drawn by the artists at the comic book company.

The artists were glad to do it for me—since I owned the company.

I stepped into my own private gold-decorated bathroom and enjoyed my huge five-spray shower.

My butler, Jives, was waiting with my clothes all laid out. And he had all three of my TVs tuned to my favorite show. Jives is an excellent fellow. I don't know how I ever did without him.

After breakfast with Annette and my parents—and by the way, our cook, Edna, makes fantastic eggs—I took my limousine to school.

My driver, Tony, is careful never to run anyone over unless I tell him to.

On the way I used the telephone in the limo to call Annette. She was in her own limo.

"How's it going?" I asked her.

"Great," she said. "Absolutely great."

At school the principal rushed out to greet me, like he does most mornings. I shook his hand and slipped him a hundred-dollar bill. You know, for the little things he does, like moving the opening bell back two hours so I can sleep in.

A bunch of kids came running up, too.

I looked up in the sky and saw a helicopter landing on the football field.

"Ah, there's my good friend Roy," I said. "By the way, Principal, there won't be any school for the next three days. We're all going to Disney World. They're opening it just for me and all my friends. And since all of you are my friends . . ."

"Yay," they all cheered.

Just another typical day now that I am a multimillionaire.

Yep, we were all heading off to Disney World together. Me and all my friends.

And boy, did I have some excellent gross practical jokes to play on all of them!

Ha-HA!

BARF·O·RAMA

Glossary of Terms

blew magoo: *noun.* To heave, vomit, extrude, blow, or hurl. As in "I was so sick, I did the blew magoo." The origins of this phrase are lost in the mists of time.

blow: *verb.* To cause stomach contents to surge upward with great force in such a way that they force their way out of the mouth. See also *vomit, hurl, heave,* and *magoo.*

buttwurst: *noun.* Named for its resemblance to other members of the "wurst" family, such as brat and knock, the traditional buttwurst differs in that it is not accompanied by either sauerkraut or mustard.

farticane: *noun*. A fart of great and terrifying power. Farticanes often begin in the Caribbean as a result of the large number of elderly cruise ship passengers who consume excessive amounts of shipboard food.

fartillery: *noun*. Farts fired rapidly for maximum destruction.

gack dance: *noun*. The characteristic gagging that precedes an episode of hurling.

gumbo: *noun*. Not sure, but believed to involve okra.

gutsunami: *noun*. A tsunami is a tidal wave. A gutsunami is a tidal wave of barf. Physicists tell us that barf may be a wave or a particle, depending.

heave: *verb*. See *hurl*.

hurl: *verb*. To emit stomach contents in a forceful way. See also *magoo*.

karma: *noun.* The idea that what you do to others will come back at you; cosmic revenge. Bad karma means you've done a lot of rotten things, and sooner or later you'll get paid back. The Tanner twins are known to have bad karma.

maggot: *noun.* The wormlike children of flies, they generally feed on rotting food. Maggots are the only living creatures who have never been called "cute."

magoo: *1. noun.* Vomit, stomach contents, lunch revisited, gumbo. *2. verb.* To huff, hurl, chuck, extrude, vomit, heave, or blow.

ninja fart: *noun.* The ninja fart arrives silently and does its destructive work without warning.

orange ingredient: *noun.* Earwax. Ear goo. The results of ear mining.

poopfume: *noun.* The aroma of fart.

popper: *noun.* A fart that expresses itself in a loud pop. When extended over the course of several seconds, the "popper" becomes a "multipopper."

Pukatoa: *noun*. A volcano usually described as being east of Java, it is actually west of Java. Or the reverse.

regrettable fluids: According to ancient philosophers, there are five regrettable fluids. In the original Latin they are pukus, mucus, poopus, waxus earimus, and weewee.

squeezer: *noun*. A fart that makes an almost plaintive wailing sound.

universal hufferage: *noun*. When a group, party, assemblage, or nation vomits as one.

vomish: The strange language that results when a person attempts to speak while hurling.

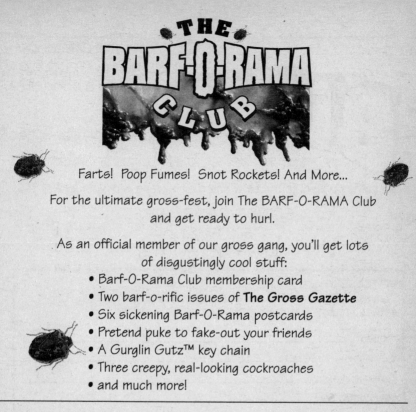

THE BARF-O-RAMA CLUB

Farts! Poop Fumes! Snot Rockets! And More...

For the ultimate gross-fest, join The BARF-O-RAMA Club
and get ready to hurl.

As an official member of our gross gang, you'll get lots
of disgustingly cool stuff:

- Barf-O-Rama Club membership card
- Two barf-o-rific issues of **The Gross Gazette**
- Six sickening Barf-O-Rama postcards
- Pretend puke to fake-out your friends
- A Gurglin Gutz™ key chain
- Three creepy, real-looking cockroaches
- and much more!

Join the BARF-O-RAMA Club for the one year membership fee of only $5.50 for U.S. residents, $7.50 for Canadian residents (U.S. currency). Includes shipping & handling.

Send a check or money order (do not send cash) made payable to "Bantam Doubleday Dell" along with this form to:

✂ -

BARF-O-RAMA Club, PO-Box 12393, Hauppauge, NY 11788

NAME _____
(Please print clearly)

ADDRESS _____

CITY _____ STATE _____ ZIP _____
(Required)

AGE _____ BIRTHDAY _____/_____/_____

Allow 6-8 weeks after check clearance for delivery. Addresses without ZIP codes cannot be accepted and money will be returned to the sender.Offer good in USA & Canada only. Void where prohibited by law.

Q: What's the difference between rice pudding and a booger?

BLEAH!

A: No one eats rice pudding.

Fill in the consent form below and mail it, along with your joke(s), to:

BDD-BFYR/BARF JOKES
1540 Broadway
New York, NY 10036

TO BDD-BFYR/BARF JOKES:
I am sending you my grossest joke(s) for you to possibly print in *BARF-O-RAMA: THE GROSSEST GROSS JOKE BOOK*.

Signed: _____

Name (please print): _____

Street address: _____

City, State, Zip: _____

Birth date: _____/_____/_____

Parent's signature: _____

All jokes submitted become the property of Bantam Doubleday Dell's Books for Young Readers Division and can be used in any additional books, advertising, or promotion without compensation.

Your joke will be considered for publication only if your parent or guardian has signed this consent form. BDD-BFYR may use your joke with or without your name as described above.

Know any gross jokes?

Tell us your favorite joke—the grosser the better. If your joke grosses us out, it may appear in

BARF-O-RAMA: THE GROSSEST GROSS JOKE BOOK,
coming in April 1997.